D0450360

Mary Ventura and the Ninth Kingdom

Also by Sylvia Plath

POETRY

Ariel

The Colossus

Crossing the Water

Winter Trees

Collected Poems (edited by Tim Hughes)

Selected Poems (edited by Tim Hughes)

Ariel: The Restored Edition
(Foreword by Frieda Hughes)

Poems (chosen by Carol Ann Duffy)

FICTION

The Bell Jar

Johnny Panic and the Bible of Dreams

NONFICTION

The Letters of Sylvia Plath Volume 1: 1940–1956
(edited by Peter K. Steinberg and Karen Kukil)

The Letters of Sylvia Plath Volume 2: 1956–1963
(edited by Peter K. Steinberg and Karen Kukil

Letters Home: Correspondence 1950–1963
(edited by Aurelia Schober Plath)

The Journals of Sylvia Plath
(edited by Karen V. Kukil)

Sylvia Plath: Drawings (edited by Frieda Hughes)

FOR CHILDREN

The Bed Book (illustrated by Quentin Blake)

The It Doesn't Matter Suit
(illustrated by Rotraut Susanne Berner)

Collected Children's Stories
(illustrated by David Roberts)

Mary Ventura and the Ninth Kingdom

A Story

Sylvia Plath

HARPER

An Imprint of HarperCollins*Publishers*

HarperCollins books may be purchased for educational, business, or sales promotional use. For information, please email the Special Markets Department at SPsales@harpercollins.com.

Originally published in the United Kingdom in 2019 by Faber and Faber Ltd.

Library of Congress Cataloging-in-Publication Data has been applied for.

ISBN 978-0-06-294085-8 (library edition)
ISBN 978-0-06-294083-4 (pbk.)

19 20 21 22 23   ws   10 9 8 7 6 5 4 3 2 1

Mary Ventura and the Ninth Kingdom was written by Sylvia Plath in 1952, when she was a student at Smith College.

The real-life Mary Ventura was one of Plath's high-school friends. Plath had written an earlier story about her, as part of a creative writing assignment in her second year at Smith. That story, largely autobiographical, concerned a pair of old school friends who meet during the holidays, and shared nothing with this one except Ventura's name.

In December 1952 she finished writing this story – a 'vague symbolic tale', in her own description – and submitted it for publication to *Mademoiselle* magazine, whose writing prize she had recently won. It was rejected.

Almost two years later, Plath revised the story, changing its title to *Marcia Ventura and the Ninth*

Kingdom, making it less sinister, then curtailing it so significantly as to make it appear half-finished.

The version used here is the original rejected work – the richest, and in Harper's view, the best. This is its first publication. All original spellings have been retained.

Mary Ventura and the Ninth Kingdom

Red neon lights blinked automatically, and a voice grated from the loudspeaker. "Train leaving, on track three. . . train leaving for . . . train leaving . . ."

"I know that must be your train," Mary Ventura's mother said. "I'm sure it is, dear. Hurry. Do hurry now. Have you your ticket?"

"Yes, mother, I do. But do I have to go right away? So soon?"

"You know how trains are," Mary's father said. He looked anonymous in his gray felt hat, as if he were traveling incognito. "You know how trains are. They don't wait."

"Yes, father, I know."

The long black hand of the clock on the wall clipped off another minute. Everywhere there were people running to catch trains. Above them, the vault of the railroad station lifted like the dome of a huge cathedral.

"Train leaving on track three . . . train leaving for . . . train leaving . . ."

"Hurry, dear." Mrs. Ventura took Mary by the arm and propelled her through the glittering marble halls of the railroad terminal. Mary's father followed with her suitcase. Other people were hurrying to the train gate marked three. A conductor in a black uniform, his face shaded by the visor of his cap, herded the crowd in through the intricate black grillwork of the iron gate to the platform beyond.

"Mother," Mary said, halting, hearing the colossal hissing of the engine on the sunken track. "Mother, I can't go today. I simply can't. I'm not ready to take the trip yet."

"Nonsense, Mary," her father cut her short jovially. "You're just getting jittery. The trip north won't be an ordeal. You just get on the train and don't worry about another thing until you get to the end of the line. The conductor will tell you where to go then."

"Come, now, there's a good girl." Mary's mother tucked a strand of gilt blond hair up under her black velvet hat. "It will be an easy trip. Everyone has to leave home sometime. Everyone has to go away sooner or later."

Mary weakened. "Oh, well, all right." She let herself be led through the wrought iron gates, down the incline of the cement platform, where the air was thick with steam.

"Extra, extra," newsboys were crying out headlines, selling papers at the doors of the train. "Extra . . . ten thousand people sentenced . . . ten thousand more people . . ."

"There is nothing," Mary's mother crooned, "absolutely nothing for you to worry about." She pushed through the chaotic jostling crowds, and Mary followed in her wake, on to the next to the last car of the train. There was a long row of red plush seats, the color of wine in the bright light from the ceiling, and the seams of the car were riveted with brass nails.

"How about this seat, here in the middle?" Mr. Ventura didn't wait for an answer, but swung Mary's suitcase up on the rack. He stood back. Mrs. Ventura touched a handkerchief to her painted red mouth, started to say something, stopped. There was, after all, nothing left to say.

"Goodbye," Mary said with automatic fondness.

"Goodbye, dear. Have a good time, now." Mrs. Ventura leaned to give Mary a vague, preoccupied kiss.

Mr. and Mrs. Ventura turned and began moving away, then, starting back down the aisle and retreating through the open doorway. Mary waved, but already they were gone and did not see. She took the seat by the window, slipping out of her red coat first and hanging it on the brass hook next to the windowframe. The rest of the passengers were almost all settled, now, but a few were still coming down the aisle, searching for seats. A lady in a blue jacket, carrying a baby wrapped in a soiled white blanket, paused at Mary's seat for a minute, but then continued to the back of the car where there was more room.

"Is this seat taken?" The woman had come lurching down the aisle, puffing and red-faced, an earth-colored brown satchel in her hand. Her blue eyes crinkled up in a mass of wrinkles and her large, generous mouth stretched into a smile.

"No, no one's sitting here." Mary could not help smiling back. She moved closer to the window and watched the woman take off her battered brown hat and her brown cloth coat.

"Oof," sighed the woman, sinking heavily into the red plush seat, "I almost thought I wouldn't make it this trip. Train's just about to start up."

The engine gave a snort, shuddered, and paused. "Board . . . all 'board!" a voice yelled from outside. The door to the car slammed shut with a final click, closing them all in.

"This is it," the woman said. "The departure." Steam rose up beyond the windowpane as the train slowly chugged down the track, and they could not see beyond the clouds of smoke and cinders.

The woman reached into her satchel and

pulled out some knitting, the beginnings of a soft fabric of leaf-green wool.

"Oh," Mary exclaimed. "How pretty. What's it going to be?"

"A dress, eventually." The woman appraised Mary with half-shut eyes. "For a girl just about your size, too."

"I'm sure she'll just love it."

The woman looked at Mary with an amused smile. "I hope so," she said, and fell silent.

The train was still hurtling through the black tunnel when the squabble started on the seat in front of them. Two little boys were sitting there, across the aisle from their mother who was reading a magazine. They were playing with tin soldiers.

"Give me that," the bigger boy with the black eyes said to his brother. "That's my soldier. You took my soldier."

"I did not," the pale tow-headed fellow said. "I did not take it."

"You did too. I saw you." The older boy picked up a tin soldier and struck his brother on the forehead. "There! Serves you right."

Blood oozed from a purpling bruise. The younger boy began to whimper. "I hate you," he whined. "I hate you."

The mother kept on reading her magazine.

"Here, here, that's enough," said the woman beside Mary, leaning forward over the back of the seat. She reached out to dab gently at the blood on the young boy's forehead with the hem of her white linen handkerchief. "You boys ought to be ashamed of yourselves, making all that fuss for no reason at all. Over a couple of silly tin soldiers."

The little boys pouted sullenly at the interference and began to play quietly again.

The woman leaned back. "I don't know what's the trouble with children these days. They seem to get worse and worse." She sighed, and took up her knitting again. Outside there was a sudden increase of light.

"Look," said Mary. "We've come out of the tunnel."

The train had shot into the somber gray afternoon, and the bleak autumn fields stretched away on either side of the tracks beyond the cinder beds. In the sky hung a flat orange disc that was the sun.

"The air is so thick and smoky!" Mary exclaimed. "I've never seen the sun that strange color before."

"It's the forest fires," the woman replied. "The smoke always blows down from the north this time of year. We'll be getting into more of it later on."

A wooden shack with boarded windows sprang up beside the tracks and dwindled off into the distance.

"What is that house doing out here so far away from everything?"

"That wasn't a house. It used to be the first station on the line, but now they don't use it much any more, so it is all shut up. This trip has gotten to be pretty much of an express."

Lulled by the clocking rhythm of the train wheels, Mary stared out of the window. In one of the corn fields a scarecrow caught her eye, crossed staves propped aslant, and the corn husks rotting under it. The dark ragged coat wavered in the wind, empty, without substance. And below the ridiculous figure black crows were strutting to and fro, pecking for grains in the dry ground.

The train sped on. "I think I will get a cup

of coffee in the dining car," the woman was saying to Mary, then. "Want to come?"

"Sure," said Mary. "Sure, I'd like to stretch my legs."

The two of them got up and walked down the aisle to the car ahead. It was the smoker, and the thick air stung Mary's eyes. Card tables were set up by the windows, and most of the men were playing poker. Waiters in white coats glided up and down with trays, serving drinks. There was the sound of loud laughter, and the clinking of ice cubes in glasses.

"Next car is the diner," the woman tossed back over her shoulder. She pushed through the door, across the swaying platform, and into the car ahead with Mary close behind.

On red plush lounges the diners reclined, eating apples and plums and hothouse grapes from the bowls of fruit on the polished wooden tables. Languid dinner music drifted from a loudspeaker concealed somewhere in the wall.

The woman stopped at a table for two and signaled Mary to sit down.

"May I take your order?" queried the black waiter in the white tailored suit, the pencil poised in his hand above a tablet of paper. Mary had not even seen him approach. He had brought ice water for each of them.

"I think I would like a glass of ginger ale," Mary said.

"I'll have the usual," the woman smiled at him.

"Sure thing . . . coffee, cream, and sugar." The black waiter flashed the woman a grin and scribbled hieroglyphics on his paper tablet.

The order came, the coffee steaming in a glazed green pottery cup and the ginger ale, shot through with small silver bubbles, in a tall glass with a red cherry at the bottom.

"How delicious !" Mary cried. "I've never eaten in a dining car before. It's so luxurious."

"Yes," the woman agreed, warming her hands about the cup of steaming brown liquid. "Yes, they do their best to make the ride as pleasant as possible."

Mary relaxed in the soft ease, sipping her ginger ale. In the subtle indirect light, the cushioned seats were a warm red color, and the music came lilting continually from the hidden loudspeaker. Mary sucked up the last of her ginger ale and tipped the glass so that the cherry rolled down into her hand. She popped it into her mouth and bit into the sweet fruit.

Outside the picture window the orange sun was sinking in the gray west. It seemed smaller than when Mary had last looked at it, and the orange color was deepening into red.

"Goodness, it's getting late fast," Mary remarked, gazing out at the barren, darkening landscape.

"One hardly notices the time go by on this trip," the woman nodded. "It is so comfortable here inside the train. But we have just passed the fifth stop along the way and that means we'll be going into the long tunnel soon. Shall we go back to the car?"

"Yes, let's. Do we pay now?"

"No," the woman told her. "They will just add the amount on to your bill at the end of the trip." She rose and started back to the car, planting her feet firmly, one after the other, on the swaying aisle of the speeding train.

Back in their seats, the woman took up her knitting again, and Mary idly watched the sterile farmlands going past. At the end of the car, the baby began to cry, spoiled and petulant. Three businessmen came down the aisle from the cocktail bar, lurching with the motion of the train and laughing. The lights in the ceiling were hard glaring stars.

"Damn brat," one man said.

"Yeah, you're not kidding," said the second man. And under their gray felt hats all three men were exactly alike. Blundering, lurching, they shouldered through the car, and the baby kept on crying as if it would cry forever.

The train shot into another subway tunnel, then. Dark rocks bulked silent and swift past the window, and the wheels clocked away like the cogs of a gigantic clock.

A vendor opened the door at the front of the car and came swinging slowly along the aisle, crying "Candy, pop-corn, cash-you nuts . . . get your candy, pop-corn, cash-you nuts. . ."

"Here," said the woman, opening her brown satchel and taking out a worn purse, "I'll get us both a chocolate bar . . ."

"Oh, no," Mary protested. "Please, I'll pay for it."

"Nonsense, dear," the woman said. "This is my treat. The chocolate will be good for your sweet tooth. Besides, you'll have enough to pay for by the end of the trip."

The vendor stopped at their seat and pushed his red cap back on his forehead, sticking his thumbs in his red-and-white striped silk vest.

"What'll it be?" he began in a routine, bored voice, "We have . . ." He paused, looked closely at the woman, then, and burst out into raucous laughter.

"You making this trip again?" His voice dropped to a low, confidential tone. "There's nothing for you in this load, you know. The whole deal is signed, sealed, and delivered. Signed, sealed, and delivered."

"Don't be too sure, Bert," the woman smiled amiably. "Even bookkeepers can go wrong, now and then."

"Bookkeepers, maybe, but not the boss." Bert jingled his black change purse with a sly grin. "The boss has got his all sewed up. Personally, this time, personally."

The woman broke into rich laughter. "Yes, I should think so, after the mistake he made on the last trip, getting the trains crossed on the higher level. Why, he couldn't get those people out of the lower gardens now if he tried. They took to the gardens like children, happy as larks. You think they'd obey him and go back on the lower subway where they belong? Not on your life."

Bert screwed his face up like a monkey. "Yeah," he said, subdued. "Yeah, I suppose you gotta get some percentage some of the time."

"That's why I'm here," the woman said. "I'll take a chocolate bar."

"Large or small."

"Large," the woman replied, and handed him a quarter.

"Well, bye now," Bert said, touching his cap. "Happy hunting," and he swung off down the aisle, calling in a bored singsong, "Candy, pop-corn, cash-you nuts . . ."

"Poor Bert," the woman remarked to Mary, unwrapping the chocolate bar without tearing the fragile silver foil. "He gets so lonely for someone to talk to on this run. It's such a long trip that hardly anybody makes it twice." She broke a section from the chocolate bar and handed a large piece of the flat brown candy to Mary. The smell of the chocolate rose rich and fragrant.

"Mmm," said Mary. "It smells good." She took a bite and let the candy dissolve on her tongue, sucking at the sweetness and letting the syrup run down her throat.

"You seem to know a lot about this trip," Mary said to the woman. "Do you travel a great deal?"

"Goodness, yes. I've been traveling here and there as long as I can remember. But I make this trip most often."

"I shouldn't wonder. It *is* a comfortable ride, really. They do so many nice extra little things, like the refreshments every hour, and the drinks in the card room, and the lounges in the dining car. It's almost as good as a hotel."

The woman flashed her a sharp look. "Yes, my dear," she said dryly, "but remember you pay for it. You pay for it all in the end. It's their business to make the trip attractive. The train company has more than a pure friendly interest in the passengers."

"I suppose you're right," Mary admitted with a laugh. "I hadn't thought about it that way. But tell me, what will it be like when we get off the train? I can't imagine. The travel folders don't say anything about the climate, or the people in the north country, nothing at all."

The woman bent over her knitting, suddenly intent. There was a knot in the thread. Swiftly, she straightened out the wool and went on stitching.

"You're going to the end of the line, I take it," she said.

"That's right, the end of the line. Father said I didn't have to worry about connections or anything, and that the conductor would tell me where to go from there."

"The last station," the woman murmured. "Are you sure?"

"Yes. At least that's what it says on my ticket. It is such a strange ticket that I remembered the number, red on black. The ninth kingdom, it said. That's a funny way to label railroad stations."

"One gets used to it after a while," the woman said, as if talking to herself. "And to all the absurd little divisions and subdivisions and classifications. Arbitrary, that's what it is. Arbitrary. But nobody seems to realize that nowadays. One little motion, one positive gesture, and the whole structure would collapse, fall quite apart."

"I don't quite see what you mean," said Mary.

"Of course not, of course not, my dear. I quite forgot myself. I was talking in circles. But tell me, have you noticed, just as you sit here, anything at all unusual about the people on this train?"

"Why no," Mary said slowly, looking around. "Why no," she repeated, puzzled. "They look all right to me."

The woman sighed. "I guess I'm just overly sensitive," she said.

Red neon blinked outside the window, and the train slowed, shuddering into the station of the sixth kingdom. The car door swung open, and the tread of the conductor came down the aisle to the blond woman up ahead with the red painted mouth, who paled, drew her furs about her and shrank back.

"Not yet," she said. "Please, not yet. This is not my stop. Give me a little longer."

"Let me see your ticket," the conductor said, and the woman wet her lips, the color of blood.

"I mislaid it. I can't find it," she said.

"It is in the second finger of your right glove," the conductor said tonelessly, "where you hid it as I came in."

Angrily the woman jerked the glove off her right hand, scooped out the stub of red cardboard and thrust it at the conductor. With his punch he clipped the ticket, tore it across and handed her the smaller part.

"Your transfer for the river crossing," he said. "I think you had better leave now."

The woman did not move to go. The conductor put out his hand and gripped her arm. "I am sorry," he said, "but you must go now. We can't have any dallying around on this train. We have a schedule to keep. We have a quota of passengers."

"I'm coming," the woman pouted sullenly. "But let go my arm. It hurts. It burns."

"She got up and walked down the aisle, her crimson wool skirt balancing and swaying about her legs, her head held proud and defiant. Outside the door of the car, on the platform, there were two station guards waiting for her. In the red glare of neon light that fell full upon them, they took the woman away, one on either side of her, through the barred exit gate.

The conductor came back down the car, wiping his forehead with a large red silk handkerchief. He paused at Mary's seat and grinned at the woman. His eyes were black, bottomless, but flecked now with cold spots of laughter.

"We don't usually have that much trouble with the passengers when their stop comes," he said to the woman.

She smiled back at him, but her voice was tender, regretful. "No, they generally don't protest at all. They just accept it when the times comes."

"Accept what?" Mary stared curiously at the two of them, remembering the frightened face of the blond woman, her mouth wet, the bright color of blood.

The conductor winked at the woman and walked away down the aisle, with the lights burning in the sockets of the walls like candles and the metal vault of the car arching overhead. The red light of the station slanted through the car windows and briefly stained the faces of the passengers scarlet. Then the train started up again.

"Accept what?" Mary pursued. She gave an involuntary shiver as if struck by a sudden chill draft of air.

"Are you cold, dear?"

"No," said Mary. "Accept what?"

"The destination," the woman replied, picking up the knitting from her lap and beginning again to add to the mesh of leaf-green wool. Expertly she jabbed the needle into the growing fabric, caught a loop of thread, and slipped it off on the needle. Mary stared at the competent, deft-moving hands. "The passengers buy their tickets," the woman went on, counting silently the stitches on the needle. "They buy their tickets, and they are responsible for getting off at the proper station. . . They choose the train, and the track, and travel to their destination."

"I know. But that woman. She looked so frightened."

"Yes, sometimes the passengers are like that. Last minute jitters, you know. The awareness strikes them too late, and they regret buying the ticket. Regret doesn't help, though. They should have thought about taking the trip beforehand."

"I still don't see why she couldn't have changed her mind and not gotten off. She could have paid more at the end of the ride."

"The railroad company doesn't allow that on this trip," the woman said. "It would create confusion."

Mary sighed, "Well, at least the rest of the passengers seem content enough."

"Yes, don't they. That is the horror of it."

"Horror?" Mary's voice rose. "What do you mean, horror? You make everything sound so mysterious."

"It's really quite simple. The passengers are so blasé, so apathetic that they don't even care about where they are going. They won't care until the time comes, in the ninth kingdom."

"But what *is* the ninth kingdom?" Mary cried petulantly, her face anguished, as if she were about to burst into tears. "What is so awful about the ninth kingdom?"

"There, there," the woman comforted, "have some more of my chocolate bar. I can't finish it all myself." Mary took a piece and put it in her mouth, but the taste was bitter on her tongue.

"You will be happier if you do not know," the woman said gently. "It is really not too bad, once you get there. The trip is long down the tunnel, and the climate changes gradually. The hurt is not intense when one is hardened to the cold. Look out the window. Ice has begun to form on the subway walls, and no one has even noticed or complained."

Mary stared out of the window at the black walls hurtling past. There were gray streams of ice between the cracks in the stones. The frozen surface caught the light from the car and glittered as if full of cold silver needles.

Mary shuddered. "I would never have come if I had known. I won't stay. I won't," she exclaimed. "I will get the next train back home."

"There are no return trips on this line," the woman said softly. "Once you get to the ninth kingdom, there is no going back. It is the kingdom of negation, of the frozen will. It has many names."

"I don't care. I will get off at the next stop. I won't stay on the train with these horrid people. Don't they know, don't they care where they are going?"

"They are blind," the woman said, looking steadily at Mary. "They are all quite blind."

"And you," Mary cried, turning on the woman angrily, "I suppose you are blind, too!" Her voice spiralled high and shrill, but no one paid any attention. No one turned to look at her.

"No," the woman said, suddenly tender, "not blind. Nor deaf. But I do happen to know that the train will make no more stops. No more stops are scheduled until we arrive at the ninth kingdom."

"But you don't understand." Mary's

face crumpled and she began to cry. Tears dropped wet and scalding through her fingers. "You don't understand. It's not my fault I took this train. It was my parents. They wanted me to go."

"You let them buy the ticket for you, though," the woman persisted. "You let them put you on the train, didn't you? You accepted and did not rebel."

"It's still not my fault," Mary exclaimed vehemently, but the woman's eyes were upon her, level after blue level of reproach, and Mary felt herself sinking, drowned in shame. The shuttle of the train wheels struck doom into her brain. Guilt, the train wheels clucked like round black birds, and guilt, and guilt, and guilt.

Guilt, said the click of the knitting needles. "You don't understand," Mary began again. "Please, let me explain. I tried to stay at home. I didn't want to come really at all. Even in the station I wanted to go back."

"But you didn't go back," the woman said, and as she caught and looped the green wool, her eyes were sad. "You chose not to go back, and now there is nothing you can do about it."

Mary sat suddenly upright, glaring through her tears. "Oh, yes there is!" she said defiantly. "There *is* still something I can do. I am going to get off anyway, while there is still time. I am going to pull the emergency cord."

The woman flashed Mary a sudden radiant smile, and her eyes lit with admiration. "Ah," she whispered, "good. You are a spunky one. You have hit upon it. That is the one trick left. The one assertion of the will remaining. I thought that, too, was frozen. There is a chance now."

"What do you mean?" Mary drew back suspiciously. "What do you mean, a chance?"

"A chance to escape. Listen, we are nearing the seventh station. I know this trip well. There is time yet. I will tell you the best moment to pull the cord, and then you must run. The platform of the station will be deserted. They were expecting no incoming or outgoing passengers this trip."

"How do you know? How can I believe you?"

"Ah, faithless child," the woman's voice was rich with tenderness. "I have been on your side all along. But I could not tell you. I could not help you until you had made the first positive decision. That is one of the rules."

"Rules, what rules?"

"The rules in the book of the train company. Every organization has to have bylaws, yon know. Certain commandments to make things run smoothly."

The woman continued. "We are approaching the station of the seventh kingdom. You must walk down the aisle to the back of the car. No one will be watching. Pull the cord from there, and don't hesitate, no matter what. Just run."

"But you," Mary said. "Aren't you coming, too?"

"I? I cannot come with you. You must make the break yourself, but be certain, I will see you soon."

"But how? I don't see how. You said there is no return trip. You said no one ever leaves the ninth kingdom."

"There are exceptions," the woman said smiling. "I do not need to obey all the laws. Only the natural ones. But you must hurry.

The station approaches, and it is time."

"Wait, just a minute. I must get my suitcase. I have all my things in it."

"Leave your suitcase," the woman instructed. "You will not need it. It would only hinder you. But remember, run, run like the wind." Her voice dropped. "There will be a brightly lighted gateway. Do not take that. Go up the stairs, even if they look black, even if there are lizards. Trust me, and take the stairway?"

"Yes," said Mary, standing up, sliding across in front of the woman and out into the aisle. "Yes."

She began to walk slowly, casually to the back of the car. There was no one watching her. At the end of the aisle, she reached over and pulled the cord labelled "Emergency" that was nailed along the length of the wall.

At once the terrible siren began to shriek through the train, splitting the silence apart. Mary flung the door open and slipped out on to the swaying platform between the two cars. There was a grinding of gears, a screech of metal careening upon metal, and the train lurched to a stop.

It was the platform of the seventh kingdom, and it was deserted. Mary cleared the three steps of the train in one leap, and the cement floor struck up with a shot of pain under the soles of her feet. There were shouts, now, of the conductors on the train.

"Hey, Ron, what's the matter?" The voice was hoarse. Red lanterns flared through the cars.

"Matter, Al? I thought it was you."

Ahead was a gateway, studded with brilliant red neon lights, and there was jazz coming syncopated from the distance, beckoning. No, not the gate. To the right an unlighted stairway rose, menacing and narrow. Mary turned and ran toward it, the echo ricocheting back from the stone walls. Under her ribs the breath was caught, tight and hurting. The shouts were louder now.

"Look! It's a girl. She's getting away!"

"Catch her, quick!" Red light spilled after her, flooding closer.

"The boss'll fire us if we lose a soul this trip!"

Mary paused a second at the bottom of the flight of stairs and glanced back. The windows of the train were gilt squares, and the faces staring out were bored, cadaverous, impersonal. Only the conductors were running down the steps of the train after her, their faces red in the glare of neon from the gateway, their fiery lanterns swinging, smoking.

A scream caught at her throat. She turned to run up the stairs, dark, steep stairs that twisted upward. A cobweb stung her cheek, but she ran on, stumbling, scratching her fingers against the rough stone walls. Small and swift, a snake darted from a chink in one of the steps. She felt it coil icily about her ankle, but she kept on running.

The cries of the conductors stopped at last, growing weak in the distance, and then she heard the train start up once more, rumbling away into the frozen core of the earth with a sound like sunken thunder. Only then did she stop running.

Leaning aslant the soot-stained wall for a moment, panting like a hunted animal, she tried to swallow the slick taste of brass in her mouth. She was free.

She began again to trudge up the dark stairs, and as she climbed, the steps became broader, smoother, and the air thinned, growing lighter. Gradually the passage widened, and there came the sound, from somewhere beyond, of bells chiming in a clock tower, clear and musical. Like a link of metal, the small snake fell from her ankle and glided away into the wall.

As she rounded the next bend of the stair, the natural sunlight broke upon her in full brilliance, and she smelled the forgotten fragrance of sweet air, earth, and fresh-cut grass. Ahead was a vaulted doorway, opening out into a city park.

Mary emerged at the top of the stairs, blinking at the fertile gold webs of sunlight. White and blue pigeons rose from the pavement and circled about her head, and she heard the laughter of children playing among the leaves of the bushes. Everywhere about the park the pinnacles of the city rose in tall white granite spires, their glass windows flashing in the sun.

Like one awakening from a sleep of death, she walked along the gravel path that twinkled with the mica of the little pebbles. It was the spring of the year, and there was a woman selling flowers on the street corner, singing to herself. Mary could see the full boxes of white roses and daffodils, looped with green leaves, and the woman in a brown coat bending maternally over the display.

As Mary approached, the woman lifted her head and met Mary's eyes with a blue gaze of triumphant love. "I have been waiting for you, dear," she said.

Sylvia Plath (1932–63) was born in Boston, Massachusetts, and studied at Smith College. In 1955 she went to Cambridge University on a Fulbright scholarship, where she met and later married Ted Hughes. She published one collection of poems in her lifetime, *The Colossus* (1960), and a novel, *The Bell Jar* (1963). Her *Collected Poems*, which contains her poetry written from 1956 until her death, was published in 1981 and was awarded the Pulitzer Prize for poetry.

ALSO BY SYLVIA PLATH

THE BELL JAR
Available in Hardcover, Paperback, Large Print, eBook, Digital Audio, and CD

"An enchanting book. The author wears her scholarship with grace, and the amazing story she has to tell is recounted with humor and understanding." — *Atlantic Monthly*

Sylvia Plath's shocking, realistic, and intensely emotional novel about a woman falling into the grip of insanity. A deep penetration into the darkest and most harrowing corners of the human psyche, *The Bell Jar* is an extraordinary accomplishment and a haunting American classic.

THE COLLECTED POEMS
Available in Paperback and eBook

Pulitzer Prize winner Sylvia Plath's complete poetic works, edited and introduced by Ted Hughes.

ARIEL
Poems
Available in Paperback

Sylvia Plath's celebrated collection.

When Sylvia Plath died, she not only left behind a prolific life but also her unpublished literary masterpiece, *Ariel*. Her husband, Ted Hughes, brought the collection to life in 1966, and its publication garnered worldwide acclaim. This collection showcases the beloved poet's brilliant, provoking, and always moving poems, including "Ariel" and once again shows why readers have fallen in love with her work throughout the generations.

ARIEL: THE RESTORED EDITION
A Facsimile of Plath's Manuscript, Reinstating Her Original Selection and Arrangement
Available in Hardcover, Paperback, and eBook

Sylvia Plath's famous collection, as she intended it.

This facsimile edition restores, for the first time, Plath's original manuscript — including handwritten notes — and her own selection and arrangement of poems. This edition also includes in facsimile the complete working drafts of her poem "Ariel," which provide a rare glimpse into the creative process of a beloved writer.

WINTER TREES
Poems
Available in eBook

Following themes of hope, loneliness, and despair, *Winter Trees* is a collection of poems written by Sylvia Plath during an elevated state of creativity prior to her passing in 1963.

JOHNNY PANIC AND THE BIBLE OF DREAMS
Short Stories, Prose, and Diary Excerpts
Available in Paperback and eBook
Renowned for her poetry, Sylvia Plath was also a brilliant writer of prose. This collection of short stories, essays, and diary excerpts highlights her fierce concentration on craft, the vitality of her intelligence, and the yearnings of her imagination.

CROSSING THE WATER
Transitional Poems
Available in Paperback and eBook
Crossing the Water is a 1971 posthumous collection of poetry by Sylvia Plath that was prepared for publication by Ted Hughes. These poems were written at the same time as those that appear in *Ariel*. *Crossing the Water* continues to push the envelope between dark and light, between our deep passions and desires that are often in tension with our duty to family and society. Water becomes a metaphor for the surface veneer that many of us carry, but Plath explores how easily this surface can be shaken and disturbed.

THE LETTERS OF SYLVIA PLATH VOLUME 1
1940-1956
Available in Hardcover and eBook
"Engaging and revealing, *The Letters of Sylvia Plath* offers a captivating look into the life and inner thinking of one of the most influential writers of the 20th century."
—Paul Alexander, *Washington Post*
Intimate and revealing, this masterful compilation offers fans and scholars generous and unprecedented insight into the life of one of our most significant poets.

THE LETTERS OF SYLVIA PLATH VOLUME 2
1956-1963
Available in Hardcover and eBook
"As the marriage faltered, the masks fell away . . . Plath wrote honestly of her unhappiness and fear . . . Poems were pouring out of her. It seemed impossible that she would not make it."
—Parul Sehgal, *New York Times*
The second volume in the definitive, complete collection of the letters of Pulitzer Prize-winning poet, Sylvia Plath, from the early years of her marriage to Ted Hughes to the final days leading to her suicide in 1963, many never before seen.